THE BABY-SITTERS CLUB®

MARY ANNE'S BAD LUCK MYSTERY

DON'T MISS THE OTHER
BABY-SITTERS CLUB GRAPHIC NOVELS!

KRISTY'S GREAT IDEA

THE TRUTH ABOUT STACEY

MARY ANNE SAVES THE DAY

CLAUDIA AND MEAN JANINE

DAWN AND THE IMPOSSIBLE THREE

KRISTY'S BIG DAY

BOY-CRAZY STACEY

LOGAN LIKES MARY ANNE!

CLAUDIA AND THE NEW GIRL

KRISTY AND THE SNOBS

GOOD-BYE STACEY, GOOD-BYE

JESSI'S SECRET LANGUAGE

ANN M. MARTIN

THE BABY-SITTERS CLUB®

MARY ANNE'S BAD LUCK MYSTERY

A GRAPHIC NOVEL BY

CYNTHIA YUAN CHENG

WITH COLOR BY BRADEN LAMB AND HANK JONES

An Imprint of
SCHOLASTIC

Library of Congress Control Number: 2022930698

ISBN 978-1-338-61611-8 (hardcover)
ISBN 978-1-338-61610-1 (paperback)

10 9 8 7 6 5 4 3 2 1   23 24 25 26 27

Printed in China 62
First edition, January 2023

Edited by Cassandra Pelham Fulton and David Levithan
Book design by Shivana Sookdeo
Creative Director: Phil Falco
Publisher: David Saylor

This book is for Aunt Martha and
in memory of Uncle Lyman

A. M. M.

For Mom, who provided my foundation
in both teaching kids and creating art.
For Patrick, who would play the spooky
Halloween soundtrack CD to scare me when
we were little. To all the friends I've shared my
Halloween adventures with over the years,
I've been thinking of you fondly.

C. Y. C.

KRISTY THOMAS
PRESIDENT

CLAUDIA KISHI
VICE PRESIDENT

MARY ANNE SPIER
SECRETARY

DAWN SCHAFER
TREASURER

JESSI RAMSEY
JUNIOR OFFICER

MALLORY PIKE
JUNIOR OFFICER

CHAPTER 1
YOU KNOW, I'VE BEEN THINKING...
IF I TOOK A BUNCH OF PEAS...
AND PUT THEM IN THE MASHED POTATOES...
AND SMOOSHED THEM ALL TOGETHER...
SQUICK!
IT WOULD LOOK JUST LIKE...
STOP!
STOP RIGHT THERE! I DON'T WANT TO KNOW!
squish!

DO YOU WANT TO KNOW WHAT I THINK IT WOULD SMELL LIKE?
NOOO!
THIS IS KRISTY THOMAS, MY OLDEST FRIEND AND PRESIDENT OF THE BABY-SITTERS CLUB.
WE'RE ALL MEMBERS OF THE CLUB, AND THOSE OF US IN EIGHTH GRADE ALWAYS EAT LUNCH TOGETHER AT OUR USUAL TABLE.
CLAUDIA KISHI, VICE PRESIDENT.

THAT'S ME, MARY ANNE SPIER. I'M SECRETARY.
DAWN SCHAFER, TREASURER.
MALLORY PIKE AND JESSI RAMSEY ARE JUNIOR OFFICERS. THEY'RE IN SEVENTH GRADE.
STACEY MCGILL USED TO BE OUR TREASURER, UNTIL SHE MOVED BACK TO NEW YORK. SHE STARTED A BRANCH OF THE BSC THERE!

ONE OF OUR ASSOCIATE MEMBERS, SHANNON KILBOURNE, GOES TO A DIFFERENT SCHOOL.
AND FINALLY...
OUT OF CURIOSITY, WHAT **WOULD** IT LOOK LIKE, KRISTY?
GREAT QUESTION, LOGAN!
OH PLEASE. DON'T EGG HER ON!
LOGAN BRUNO. HE'S ALSO AN ASSOCIATE MEMBER, AND MY BOYFRIEND.
LUNCH IS ONE OF MY FAVORITE TIMES OF THE DAY.

AHEM!
WHO'S GOING TO THE HALLOWEEN HOP?
IS IT TIME FOR THAT AGAIN?
OH YEAH! HALLOWEEN IS COMING UP SOON.
I LOVE THIS TIME OF YEAR.
WHY? YOU GET DRESSED UP EVERY DAY.
I'M JUST TEASING.
WELL...
LOGAN AND I ARE GOING TO THE HOP.
OOH! IN COSTUME?
WE CAN'T DECIDE. IT COULD BE FUN, THOUGH!

Psst
pst
pst
pst
COKIE MASON AND GRACE BLUME. WHAT WAS GOING ON WITH THEM?
pst
pst
yikes
ha
ha!
ARE THEY TALKING ABOUT US?
DO I HAVE SOMETHING ON MY FACE?
wipe wipe
THERE'S NOTHING ON MY SHIRT...
??

ARE THEY THE BABY-SITTERS CLUB OR THE **BABY** CLUB?
THEY THINK THEY'RE **SO** COOL, BUT THEY'RE JUST STUCK-UP.

EXCUSE ME!

COKIE, GRACE...
I DON'T THINK YOU KNOW WHAT YOU'RE TALKING ABOUT...
EVERYONE HERE WORKS VERY HARD. WHY IS THAT WORTH MAKING FUN OF US?
!
DON'T BE SO BITTER.

ARE YOU JUST EMBARRASSED BECAUSE BABY-SITTING IS OLD-FASHIONED AND UNCOOL?
ACTUALLY, RUNNING A SUCCESSFUL BUSINESS WITH YOUR BEST FRIENDS IS **VERY** COOL.
YOU WOULDN'T KNOW...
BECAUSE WITH ATTITUDES LIKE YOURS, NO ONE'S HIRING **YOU** TO DO ANY BABY-SITTING!

MARY ANNE,
YOU--!

ringggg
!

AAAAND THAT'S
THE BELL!
HOW ABOUT WE ALL
GET TO CLASS, HUH?
MARY
ANNE
SPIER!

THE WAY YOU STOOD UP FOR US WAS **GREAT**!
SO, COKIE, GRACE...
WHAT WAS THAT ABOUT BEING UNCOOL?
LET'S GO BEFORE WE'RE LATE!

CHAPTER 2

THE REST OF THE SCHOOL DAY WAS PRETTY UNEVENTFUL.
Z
LATER, I BABY-SAT FOR JAMIE, AND THEN HEADED OVER TO CLAUDIA'S HOUSE FOR OUR CLUB MEETING.
JUST A FEW MINUTES TO SPARE...
SPIER
I COULDN'T RESIST A QUICK PEEK.

I LOVE CHECKING THE MAIL. YOU NEVER KNOW WHAT YOU'LL GET!
SPIER
IT'S STUFFED!
LET'S SEE... BILLS... ADS...
Mary Anne Spier
177 Burnt Hill Rd
Stoneybrook, CT 06800
OH! A LETTER ADDRESSED TO ME!

ACK, IS THAT THE TIME?
I'M GOING TO BE LATE!
SPIER
SPIER
SPIER
HI, MIMI!
HELLO, MY MARY ANNE. HOW ARE YOU TODAY?
REALLY GOOD!
I WAS ECSTATIC ABOUT MY LETTER.

HEY, EVERYONE!
LOOK! WE WERE CHECKING OUT OUR SEVENTH-GRADE YEARBOOK.
SEEMS LIKE WE HAVE SOME TIME BEFORE THE MEETING.
I'M HERE!
GREAT.
LET'S BEGIN!
OH, I GUESS IT CAN WAIT...
ring!

6:30 TOMORROW?
LET'S SEE...DAWN IS AVAILABLE!

NEXT ORDER OF BUSINESS...

GOSH, WHEN CAN I OPEN THIS LETTER ALREADY?
ALL RIGHT, THAT'S ALL I HAD ON MY LIST --

fwip!

WHAT'S THAT?
ripp!
I GOT A MYSTERIOUS LETTER THAT I HAVEN'T HAD A CHANCE TO OPEN.
THERE'S NO RETURN ADDRESS...I WONDER WHO IT'S FROM!

Do you believe in luck? You can receive
incredibly good luck within four days
of opening this letter. All you have to
do is send this letter to twenty (20)
other people.
Even if you are not superstitious,
continuing the chain will definitely bring
good fortune upon you. One person who
sent the twenty letters, Joy Su, even
on a million dollars in the lottery
ays later.
HOWEVER
copies, you
luck. Bad
you, your
Please don't
can spread good

OH, DARN!
DARN, DARN, BORING **DARN!**
WHAT IS IT?
IT'S JUST A SILLY OLD CHAIN LETTER, THAT'S WHAT.
I HATE CHAIN LETTERS.
YOU HAVE TO SEND THEM TO EVERYONE YOU KNOW, AND THEN THEY HAVE TO SEND THEM TO EVERYONE **THEY** KNOW. IT NEVER ENDS!
I'VE HEARD OF SOME NEAT CHAIN LETTERS WHERE YOU CAN RECEIVE A MILLION POSTCARDS IN RETURN!
COULD IT BE SOMETHING SIMILAR?
hmm...

THIS LETTER IS REALLY WEIRD...
R: if you do NOT send out twenty
will break the chain of good
k will then be visited upon
ds, and loved ones.
– with your help, w
all across the wo
IT SAYS IF YOU CONTINUE THE CHAIN, YOU JUST GET GOOD LUCK.
BUT IF YOU **BREAK** IT, BAD LUCK WILL BE VISITED UPON YOU...
AND YOUR FRIENDS AND LOVED ONES.
YIKES.
PFFT.

IS IT SIGNED?
NO, AND EVERYTHING IS TYPED...

THAT STUFF'S JUST NONSENSE. WHO WOULD REALLY BELIEVE IN IT?
HOW MANY ARE YOU SUPPOSED TO SEND, ANYWAY, MARY ANNE?

TWENTY!

WELL, DON'T BOTHER SENDING ONE TO ME. I'LL JUST BREAK THE CHAIN.
DON'T WORRY.
I'M NOT GOING TO SEND ANY. I DON'T THINK I EVEN HAVE THE ADDRESSES OF TWENTY PEOPLE!

WHAT?!

SO YOU'RE GOING TO BREAK THE CHAIN? THANKS A LOT!
YEAH! IF YOU BREAK IT, BAD LUCK WILL BE VISITED UPON US, TOO!
OH, IT WILL NOT.
AT LEAST...I DON'T THINK SO.
WHAT DO YOU THINK, DAWN? SHOULD I SEND YOU A LETTER?
I WANT YOU TO SEND THE LETTER...
BUT NOT TO ME...
HA HA! SEE? YOU DON'T WANT TO DEAL WITH IT.
AND NEITHER DO I. IF I HAVE TO SEND OUT TWENTY LETTERS, I'LL JUST END UP WITH TWENTY ENEMIES!

UM...I WOULDN'T MIND GETTING THE LETTER.
ME NEITHER.

OH, COME ON, YOU TWO.

IT'S JUST SUPERSTITION. FORGET IT!

KRISTY'S RIGHT.
crumple
crumple
THIS IS JUST SUPERSTITION.
...I THINK.

Mary Anne Spier

CHAPTER 3

beep!
beep beep!
BEEP!
THUD!
OOF!
UGH...
MARY ANNE?
knock knock
IS EVERYTHING OKAY?
GOOD MORNING, DAD...
6:46
COME ON IN...

WHAT HAPPENED?
I HAD THIS DREAM WHERE I WAS CLIMBING A MOUNTAIN.
beep!
beep!
beep!
BUT THEN AN ALARM RANG!
AND THEN...
beep! beep!
YOU FELL OFF THE MOUNTAIN?
YEAH! HOW DID YOU KNOW?
I'VE HAD SOME STRANGE DREAMS MYSELF.

ALL GOOD NOW?
YEAH...JUST EMBARRASSED.
WHY DON'T YOU GET READY, AND I'LL MAKE PANCAKES?
OH, SUPER!
MROOOWRR...
AW, TIGGER, YOU FRAIDY-CAT.
THUMP!
COME ON OUT, THERE'S NOTHING TO BE SCARED OF --
MRROWR!
SORRY, SORRY.

BREAKFAST SMELLS AMAZING!
I HOPE YOU ENJOY IT.
MMM, PANCAKES AND BACON!
THANKS, DAD!
!

OH NO!!
DAD, I'M SORRY! REALLY, I AM!
I KNOW YOU SAID A WHITE DRESS ISN'T PRACTICAL FOR SCHOOL.
BUT I'VE WORN IT FIVE OTHER TIMES AND IT WAS OKAY THEN --
MARY ANNE.
IT'S ALL RIGHT. HERE.
I'LL CLEAN UP. YOU GO CHANGE AND SOAK YOUR DRESS IN COLD WATER.
I'LL KEEP YOUR BREAKFAST WARM.

AFTER ALL THAT, I MET CLAUDIA OUTSIDE.

ON THE WAY TO SCHOOL, I TOLD HER ABOUT THE MORNING I WAS HAVING.

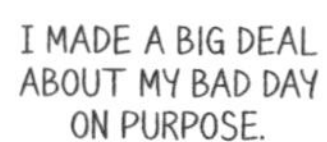

I MADE A BIG DEAL ABOUT MY BAD DAY ON PURPOSE.

MY HOPE WAS THAT IF I COMPLAINED TO CLAUDIA, NOT A SINGLE OTHER THING WOULD GO WRONG!

IT DIDN'T WORK.
??

I HAD TO GO FIND MR. HALPRIN, THE JANITOR, AND ASK HIM TO OPEN MY LOCKER FOR ME.

IN MATH CLASS, I REALIZED I'D LEFT MY HOMEWORK RIGHT WHERE I'D DONE IT.
AT HOME.
THEN AT LUNCH...
!
slosh
WET FLOOR
THANKS AGAIN, MR. HALPRIN.

BUT SPILLING MAC AND CHEESE WASN'T THE WORST PART OF THE DAY.
SO, IS MR. HALPRIN A CLOSE, PERSONAL FRIEND OF YOURS?
HA.
HA.
HEY, LIGHTEN UP!
EASY FOR YOU TO SAY.
MARY AAANNE.
WHAAAT!
GEEZ.
TOUCHY, TOUCHY.

WELL, HOW WOULD YOU FEEL IF YOU DROPPED YOUR LUNCH IN FRONT OF THE WHOLE CAFETERIA?
NOT THAT MANY PEOPLE SAW.

OH, NO.
ONLY ABOUT THREE HUNDRED!
N HOP
THAT AFTERNOON, I WALKED HOME FROM SCHOOL BY MYSELF.

I CURLED UP WITH MY FAVORITE BOOK, *LITTLE WOMEN*, WHICH MADE ME FEEL BETTER.
RING!
HELLO?
HI, MARY ANNE? THIS IS MRS. NEWTON. UM...IS EVERYTHING OKAY?
SURE, WHY?
IT'S JUST THAT YOU'RE NEVER LATE.
I'M SO SORRY!
I'LL COME RIGHT OVER!
I COULDN'T BELIEVE I'D FORGOTTEN ABOUT A BABY-SITTING JOB!
IT WAS A GOOD THING I DIDN'T BELIEVE IN SUPERSTITION, OR I MIGHT HAVE BLAMED SUCH A BAD DAY ON THE CHAIN LETTER.

WEDNESDAY

DON'T LAUGH EVERYBODY. LOOKING BACK ON IT, I CAN
SEE THAT IT WASN'T THE BEST IDEA.

I BABY-SAT FOR JACKIE RODOWSKY AND HE AND I
TRIED TO MAKE HIS HALLOWEEN COSTUME. RIDICULOUS
IDEA, HUH? YOU GOT IT.

IT WAS ONE OF THOSE DAYS WHEN I WAS SITTING FOR
JUST JACKIE BECAUSE HIS BROTHERS WERE OFF
TAKING LESSONS (PIANO FOR SHEA, AND TUMBLING
FOR ARCHIE, I THINK). ANYWAY, AS YOU KNOW, JACKIE
ALONE IS ABOUT AS MUCH TROUBLE AS ALL THREE
BOYS TOGETHER. BUT FOR SOME REASON, I WASN'T
REMEMBERING THAT, SO WHEN JACKIE ASKED TO MAKE
HIS HALLOWEEN COSTUME, I AGREED TO IT. AND THE
REST GOES DOWN IN BABY-SITTING HISTORY...

\- DAWN

CHAPTER 4
DAWN?
I WANT TO BE A ROBOT FOR HALLOWEEN!
CAN WE MAKE MY COSTUME THIS AFTERNOON?
WELL...I DON'T SEE WHY NOT.
YES!
C'MON, WE'LL MAKE IT IN THE GARAGE!
WHAT ARE WE MAKING THE COSTUME OUT OF?
BOXES AND JAR LIDS AND SPRINGS AND BUTTONS AND GOOGLY EYES.
THEN WE'LL PAINT IT!

WE CAN USE ANY OF THESE EMPTY BOXES.
ARE YOU SURE?
YEAH! LET'S USE THIS BIG ONE.
JACKIE, WAIT!

THUD!
THUD!
CRASH!
BOY, I'M GLAD THESE ARE EMPTY.
THAT WAS FUN!!

OKAY, WHAT DO
WE NEED NEXT?

PAINT!
AND STUFF.
...
OKAY, I BETTER
GET THAT.

SCRAPS

JACKIE'S FINDS:
wooden
spools
old
slinky toy
coil of
wire
jar lids
AND...

SEE? THEY'RE GOOGLY.

LAST THING IS BUTTONS.
THEY'RE UPSTAIRS IN MOM'S SEWING CHEST!
OKAY.
SCRAPS
AT LEAST HE CAN'T GET INTO MUCH TROUBLE WITH BUTTONS.
SCRAPS
KER-RASH!
JACKIE?!
OOPS.

IN CASE OF ANY STRAY NEEDLES.
VRRR

NOW WE CAN FINALLY GET STARTED ON THIS ROBOT!
I'M GOING TO MAKE THE BODY WITH THE BOXES.
OW!

ALL RIGHT.
TRY TO BE EXTRA CAREFUL FROM HERE ON OUT, OKAY?
PROMISE.
WHOOPS.
WHOOPS!
IT'S DONE!

I KNOW! I'LL PUT IT ON FOR MY MOM AND BROTHERS TO SEE!
GOOD IDEA!
TA-DA!
on
off
OH!
on
off
HUH?
on
off
OH NO!
OOPS.
I GUESS THE GLUE WASN'T DRY. POOR OLD ROBOT.

WHAT BAD LUCK.
COULD THIS BE BECAUSE MARY ANNE BROKE THE CHAIN?
AND SINCE I'M ONE OF HER FRIENDS...
BAD LUCK IS VISITING ME?
HA, NO WAY.
JACKIE ALWAYS HAS BAD LUCK!

on
off

CHAPTER 5

ANOTHER FRIDAY, ANOTHER CLUB MEETING.
I CHECKED OUR MAIL BEFORE GOING TO CLAUDIA'S. A SMALL PACKAGE WAS INSIDE!
IT'S PROBABLY FOR DAD.
BUT IT COULD BE FOR ME.
MAYBE A FREE SAMPLE, LIKE HAND LOTION?

!
BA-NG!
?
WHAT'S UP, MARY ANNE?
LOOK AT THIS!!
Mary Anne & The Baby-Sitters Club

IT LOOKS LIKE A RANSOM NOTE! CREEPY!
AND IT'S ADDRESSED NOT ONLY TO YOU, BUT THE ENTIRE CLUB...
ALL RIGHT, WE'LL JUST TAKE PHONE CALLS TODAY.
WE CAN HANDLE OFFICIAL BUSINESS ON MONDAY.
THIS PACKAGE IS MOST IMPORTANT RIGHT NOW.
YEAH...
SO WHO'S GOING TO OPEN IT?
YOU, OF COURSE!

IT'S ADDRESSED MOSTLY TO YOU.
YOU'RE SCARED!
YOU'RE RIGHT.

FINE.

!

IT'S JUST A HARMLESS JEWELRY BOX.

WE'VE BEEN AFRAID OF SOME JEWELRY.
HANG ON, ANYTHING COULD BE INSIDE!
AND THERE ARE A LOT OF **ANYTHINGS** THAT I WOULDN'T WANT TO BE ANYWHERE NEAR.

THAT'S TRUE...

TISSUE PAPER...

CLAUDIA, DO YOU HAVE SOME TWEEZERS I CAN BORROW?
OH, FOR HEAVEN'S SAKE.

TOSS!
EW!!
!!
AUGH!

!
WH-WHAT'S INSIDE?

IT LOOKS LIKE A NECKLACE.
IT'S PRETTY. I LIKE IT.
THERE'S SOME KIND OF SEED INSIDE THE GLASS.
OH WAIT, THERE'S A NOTE, TOO!
. . .
UM...YOU ALL MIGHT WANT TO TAKE A LOOK AT THIS.

HERE.
HALLOWEEN
IS COMING.
BEWARE OF
EVIL FORCES.
WEAR THIS
BAD LUCK CHARM
MARY ANNE-
OR ELSE.

AUGHH!!
BAD-LUCK CHARM?!
I KNEW IT. I JUST KNEW IT!
OH MY GOSH, I ALREADY TOUCHED IT!

TOUCHED IT?
YOU'VE GOT TO WEAR IT.
WHAT?! NO WAY!

I THINK YOU'D BETTER.

ARE YOU GOING TO IGNORE THIS WARNING...
LIKE YOU IGNORED THE CHAIN LETTER?

UM, WELL...

WHAT DOES EVERYONE ELSE THINK?

M-MAYBE YOU OUGHT TO WEAR IT.
YEAH...

I THOUGHT YOU DIDN'T BELIEVE IN SUPERSTITIOUS STUFF!

WHAT'S UP WITH YOU GUYS?

WELL...I HAD SOME PRETTY BAD LUCK SITTING FOR JACKIE YESTERDAY.
AND I FLUNKED A SPELLING TEST.

BUT JACKIE'S ALWAYS BAD LUCK.
AND, CLAUDIA, YOU ALWAYS FLUNK SPELLING TESTS.

THIS TIME WAS WORSE THAN USUAL.
I HAVEN'T FLUNKED LATELY...

I FELL IN BALLET CLASS!
THAT NEVER HAPPENS!

I GOT IN TROUBLE FOR TALKING IN MATH.
!

I LOST MY WATCH.
?

STACEY CALLED RECENTLY, AND SHE SAID SHE BROKE HER DAD'S PAPERWEIGHT. THAT ONE HE LOVES.

WELL...
TO TELL THE TRUTH, I HAD THE WORST DAY AFTER I THREW AWAY THE CHAIN LETTER.
THIS THING REALLY SCARES ME. IT'S **BAD LUCK**.
BUT WHAT HAPPENS IF I DON'T WEAR IT? THINGS MIGHT GET WORSE.
EVIL.
BUT WHO SENT THE CHARM? AND WHY DO I HAVE TO WEAR IT?

MAYBE BECAUSE YOU WERE THE ONE WHO THREW THE CHAIN LETTER AWAY.
THIS IS YOUR BAD LUCK, AND ALL THE OTHER STUFF IS BAD LUCK BEING VISITED UPON YOUR FRIENDS.

WHAT ABOUT THAT PART THAT WARNED, "BEWARE OF EVIL FORCES"?
I THINK...WE'LL HAVE TO FIGURE OUT HOW TO WARD OFF THOSE EVIL FORCES.

WE ALL KNEW IT WOULDN'T BE EASY.

BUT WE WOULD HAVE TO DO IT.
THE QUESTION WAS: HOW?

CHAPTER 6

THE DAY AFTER I STARTED WEARING THE CHARM, I BABY-SAT FOR JAMIE NEWTON.

HE SPILLED EVERYTHING, DROPPED EVERYTHING...

AND EVEN HAD A LITTLE FALL DOWN THE STAIRS.
NOTHING SEEMED TO GO RIGHT.

AT SCHOOL ON MONDAY, THERE WAS A FIRE IN A TRASH CAN.
AN EXPLOSION IN SCIENCE LAB!
AND AN ACCIDENT IN GYM CLASS.

GLOOM...

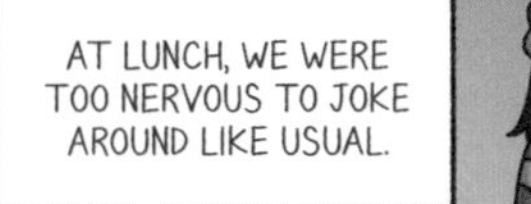

AT LUNCH, WE WERE TOO NERVOUS TO JOKE AROUND LIKE USUAL.

LOGAN WAS TAKING A MAKEUP TEST AND WASN'T THERE TO PROVIDE ANY COMFORTING WORDS.

MAYBE THIS IS ALL JUST A COINCIDENCE.
ONE LITTLE ACCIDENT MIGHT BE A COINCIDENCE.

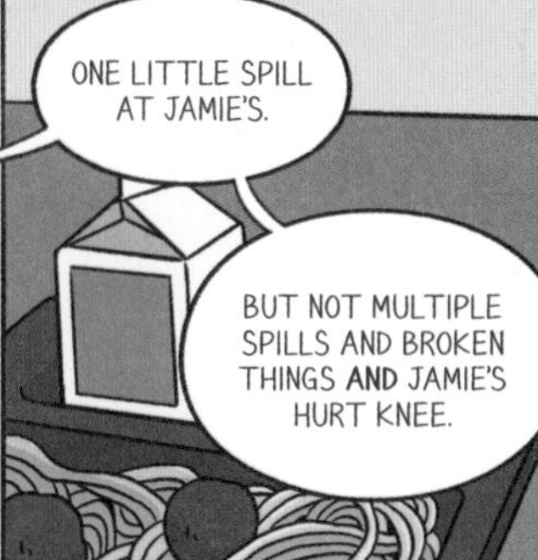

ONE LITTLE SPILL AT JAMIE'S.
BUT NOT MULTIPLE SPILLS AND BROKEN THINGS **AND** JAMIE'S HURT KNEE.

MAYBE EVEN ONE LITTLE FIRE THAT MR. HALPRIN COULD HAVE PUT OUT WITH A BUCKET OF WATER.
BUT NOT A **FIRE DEPARTMENT** FIRE...

AND AN EXPLOSION.
PLUS A GYM INJURY.

RIGHT. AND YOU KNOW WHAT?
THERE HAVE BEEN OTHER SIGNS OF BAD LUCK TODAY.

REALLY?
LIKE WHAT?
THIS MORNING...
MY FATHER OPENED AN UMBRELLA INDOORS.
BUT WAIT, THERE'S MORE!
ON THE WAY TO SCHOOL, A BLACK CAT CROSSED OUR PATH.
!
THAT'S RIGHT.
AND JUST BEFORE I GOT TO THE CAFETERIA...

I SAW A PENNY ON THE FLOOR.
I PICKED IT UP WITHOUT THINKING.
IT WAS ALREADY IN MY HAND BEFORE I REALIZED...

ONE CENT
IT WAS A TAIL-UP PENNY.
DOOM...
YOU KNOW WHAT?
THIS CHARM IS A CURSE.
AND WE HAVE TO DO SOMETHING ABOUT IT.

THAT'S WHAT MALLORY SAID ON FRIDAY. WE HAVE TO GET RID OF THE EVIL FORCES.
HOW?
...
STARE~

!
SHHH. I THINK PEOPLE ARE LISTENING.
NO WONDER.
THIS IS PROBABLY THE MOST FASCINATING CONVERSATION THEY'VE HEARD IN WEEKS.

Ha ha ha ha!
ALL RIGHT, LET'S TRY TO KEEP OUR VOICES DOWN.

SO...IT SEEMS LIKE THE CHARM COULD REALLY BE BAD LUCK.
HOW CAN WE FIND OUT MORE ABOUT CHARMS, CURSES, AND EVIL FORCES?

WE BETTER GO TO THE LIBRARY.
UGH. I HATE THE LIBRARY!

JESSI AND MAL SHOULD COME, TOO.
CLAUDIA, YOU CAN DECIDE WHAT YOU WANT TO DO.

NO. SHE'S GOING.
I AM? HOW COME?
BECAUSE THIS CLUB STICKS TOGETHER.
WE'LL MEET AT THE FRONT DOORS WHEN SCHOOL IS OVER.
END OF DISCUSSION.
THE BAD-LUCK CHARM FRIGHTENED ME, BUT I COULDN'T HELP DAYDREAMING OF THE BOOKS I'D READ ABOUT KIDS GOING ON JUST THIS SORT OF MISSION.

THEY ASK THE WHITE-HAIRED LIBRARIAN FOR BOOKS ON WITCHCRAFT.
SHE TAKES THEM TO SOME MUSTY OLD CORNER OF THE LIBRARY.
AND THEY LOOK THROUGH THE BIG, DUSTY BOOKS THAT ARE ALWAYS A LITTLE TOO HELPFUL.

WELL, OUR VISIT TO THE STONEYBROOK PUBLIC LIBRARY WASN'T ANYTHING LIKE THAT.
SO WHAT DO WE DO FIRST?
ASK THE LIBRARIAN FOR HELP?
NO, WE DON'T HAVE TO DO THAT.
READ
WE CAN JUST GO TO THE CARD CATALOG.
WE'LL FIND BETTER INFORMATION IN THE ADULT SECTION.
BUT WE HAVE TO ACT MATURE SO THE LIBRARIAN DOESN'T GET SUSPICIOUS.

I CAN'T BELIEVE THEY STILL HAVE ONE OF THESE.
NON FICTION
FLOWERS...
FOOTBALL...
WOW, THERE ARE SO MANY SUBJECTS!
WITCHCRAFT! HERE IT IS.
THIS MUST BE THE RIGHT PLACE. THIS BOOK IS CALLED *ON WITCHCRAFT*.

WITCHES THROUGH THE AGES
STRANGE PHENOMENA
CHARMS & SPELL
SO WHY DO WE NEED ALL THIS WITCH AND SPELL STUFF?
HOW ELSE WILL WE WARD OFF THE EVIL FORCES?
IT MUST BE SOME SORT OF SPELL. WE JUST HAVE TO FIGURE OUT WHICH ONE.
OKAY. A SPELL.
NONE OF US REALLY KNEW WHAT TO LOOK FOR.
BUT AT FIVE O'CLOCK, WE EACH CHOSE A BOOK TO CHECK OUT AND DASHED TO CLAUDIA'S FOR A CLUB MEETING.

Thursday

Halloween is supposed to be scary, but I never realized just how scary it can be for some little kids. I was sitting for Jamie Newton today, and it turns out that he's totally freaked-out by Halloween. Everything scares him. He's afraid of trick-or-treaters, and he's even afraid of the costume parade that's going to be held at his nursery school. (Or at least he was when I first got to his house. He didn't have a costume, either, because he said he was afraid to dress up.)

Jessi

CHAPTER 7
WELL, JAMIE, WHAT DO YOU WANT TO DO TODAY?
I WANT TO...
I WANT TO...
UM, I DON'T KNOW...
YOU WANT TO PLAY OUTSIDE?
NO!
SHUT!
TRICK-OR-TREATERS MIGHT COME BY.

OH, NOT TODAY! THERE WON'T BE ANY TRICK-OR-TREATERS UNTIL HALLOWEEN.
I HOPE IT'S NEVER HALLOWEEN.
WHAT ARE YOU SO AFRAID OF?
HALLOWEEN.
BUT HALLOWEEN IS FUN!
EVERYONE GETS CANDY, AND YOU DRESS UP.
YOU CAN BE A GHOST, OR A WITCH --
NO!
NO GHOSTS! NO WITCHES!
BUT THEY'RE JUST PEOPLE DRESSED UP, JAMIE. THEY'RE NOT REAL.
GHOSTS AND WITCHES SCARE ME.
ESPECIALLY GHOSTS.

YOU KNOW, NOT ALL GHOSTS ARE MEAN.
HAVE YOU EVER HEARD OF OLLIE?
OLLIE?
YEAH. HE WAS A GHOST -- A LITTLE ONE -- AND HE WAS VERY SHY. HE DIDN'T LIKE LOUD NOISES OR TOO MUCH CONFUSION.
HE LIVED IN THE ATTIC OF MR. AND MRS. LEI'S HOUSE.
ALL HE WANTED WAS PEACE AND QUIET. AND TO BE WITH HIS FRIENDS, PLUTO AND MISS AMELIA.
WHO ARE THE LEIS? AND WHO ARE PLUTO AND MISS AMELIA?
IF YOU'RE CURIOUS... WE CAN GO TO MY HOUSE AND LOOK AT SOME BOOKS ABOUT OLLIE.
WELL...
OKAY.
ALL RIGHT, LET'S GO!

FIRST THINGS FIRST. LET'S GET THAT JACKET ON.
JESSI, CAN YOU TIE MY SHOELACES, TOO?
OH, UM, YES!
THE BUTTON, THE SHOELACE, JAMIE'S HUGE FEAR OF HALLOWEEN...
IT'S THE BAD LUCK!

JESSI?
!

inhaaale~

?
pheww

OKAY, JAMIE.
CAN YOU SHOW ME WHERE THE SEWING BOX AND EXTRA SHOELACES ARE?

I'LL FIX YOU UP, AND THEN WE'LL GO TO MY HOUSE TO READ SOME OLLIE BOOKS.

HI, MAMA.
JAMIE NEWTON AND I ARE STOPPING BY FOR A FEW MINUTES.
HI, JAMIE.
HI.
I'LL EXPLAIN LATER.

OKAY, HERE WE GO.
OLLIE and the HALLOWEEN COSTUME
UH-OH.
NO, IT'S OKAY. REALLY.
WE'LL LOOK AT THE PICTURES FIRST, OKAY?
SEE THESE TWO PEOPLE?
ARE THEY MR. AND MRS. LEI?
THEY ARE! AND HERE ARE PLUTO AND MISS AMELIA.
A MOUSE AND A BAT?! THEY'RE SO CUTE!
AND...THIS IS OLLIE.
"Hello!" Ollie said shyly.

THAT LITTLE THING? BUT HE DOESN'T LOOK MEAN AT ALL. HE'S SMILING.
HE ISN'T MEAN, REMEMBER? LET'S KEEP GOING.
TOGETHER, THEY READ ABOUT A LITTLE GHOST WHO WAS SO SHY THAT HE WOULDN'T ENTER THE TOWN'S CONTEST FOR BEST HALLOWEEN COSTUME.
HIS FRIENDS PUT ON A CONTEST OF THEIR OWN, AND THEY NAMED OLLIE THE WINNER!
"Well, you're the winner of our costume contest!"
ALTHOUGH THERE WAS NO PRIZE, OLLIE HAD A VERY HAPPY HALLOWEEN.
THE END.
...
I WONDER IF MOMMY COULD MAKE ME AN OLLIE COSTUME.

YOU WANT TO BE A GHOST?
NO. OLLIE.
THEN, IF THERE ARE ANY CONTESTS, MAYBE I'LL WIN. AND OLLIE COULD GET HIS PRIZE AFTER ALL.
NOW THAT...
IS A GREAT IDEA.
ARE THERE ANY MORE OLLIE BOOKS?
YUP!
WELL...LET'S READ THEM!!

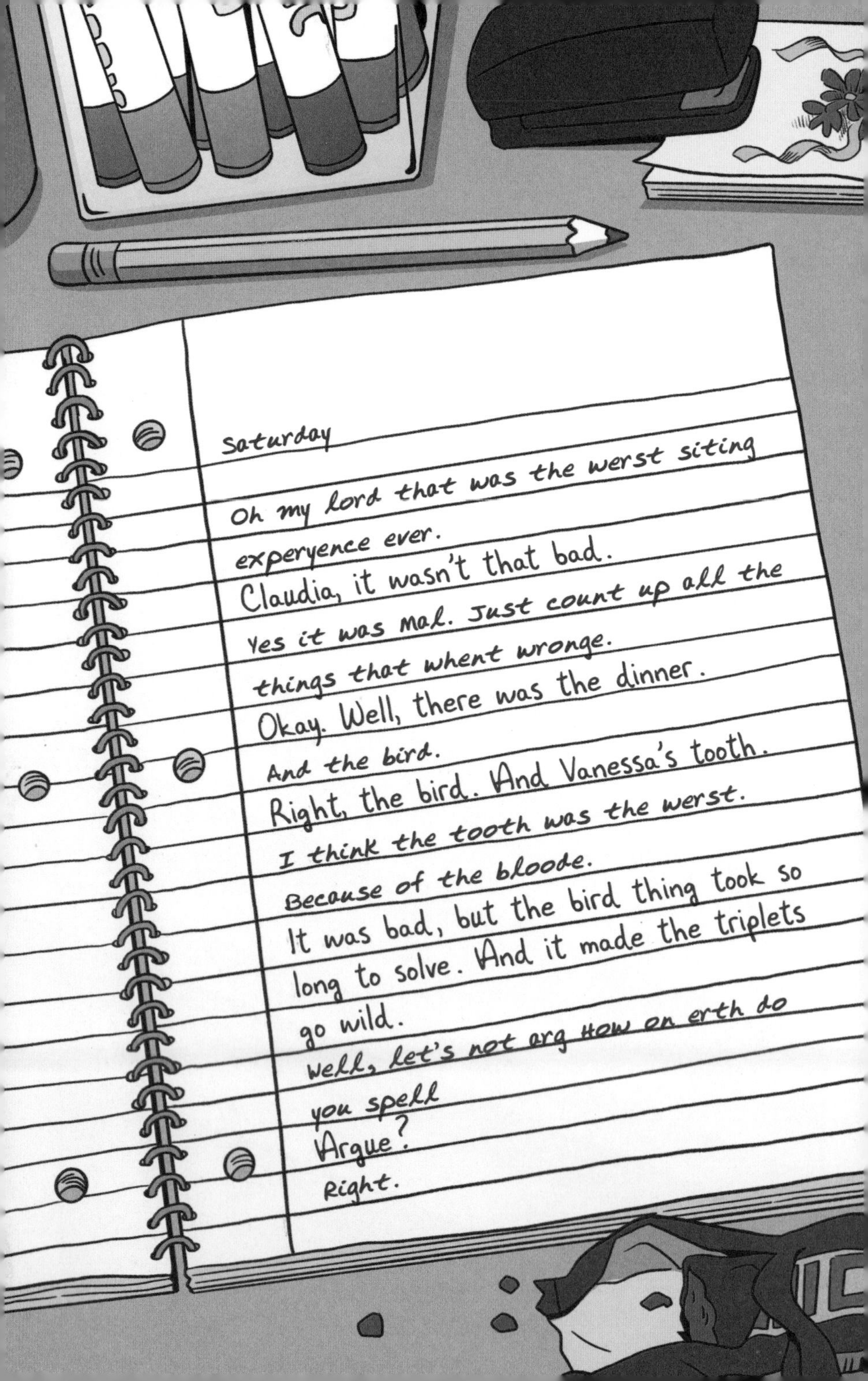
Saturday
Oh my lord that was the werst siting experyence ever.
Claudia, it wasn't that bad.
Yes it was Mal. Just count up all the things that whent wronge.
Okay. Well, there was the dinner.
And the bird.
Right, the bird. And Vanessa's tooth.
I think the tooth was the werst.
Because of the bloode.
It was bad, but the bird thing took so long to solve. And it made the triplets go wild.
Well, let's not arg How on erth do you spell
Argue?
Right.

CHAPTER 8

JUST LET THE DADDY STEW HEAT UP UNTIL 6:30 AND YOU SHOULD BE GOOD TO GO.
ALL RIGHT, YOU KIDS. HAVE FUN!
6:30! I CAN'T WAIT THAT LONG!

BYRON, THAT'S LESS THAN HALF AN HOUR FROM NOW.
noooo

I COULD FAINT BEFORE THEN!
YOU WON'T.
HELP US SET UP THE REC ROOM! TONIGHT WILL BE A LITTLE SPECIAL.

INDOOR PICNIC!!

WHAT'S THAT SMELL?

SOMETHING BURNING?

WHERE'S BYRON?

!!
hiss!
OOPS...
off!

EW! YUCK!
PEE-YEW!
THE DADDY STEW IS RUINED, MALLORY. BYRON RUINED IT.
YUCK!
I'M SORRY. HONEST.
I WAS HUNGRY. I JUST THOUGHT THAT IF I TURNED THE FIRE UP...
AUUGH!
NOW WHAT?
I DON'T KNOW...
BUT THAT SOUNDS LIKE MORE THAN A STOP-TEASING-ME-OR-ELSE SCREAM.
WAUGH!
WE'LL GO CHECK. STAY AWAY FROM THE STOVE, BYRON!

OH MY GOSH!! WHERE DID THAT COME FROM?!
WAHH!
IT FLEW DOWN THE CHIMNEY!
AUGHH! HELP!!
chirp!!
HANG ON AND CALM DOWN, EVERYONE!
THAT BIRD IS SCARED AND YOU'RE SCARING IT EVEN MORE.
HOW ARE WE GOING TO CATCH IT?

MAYBE IF WE OPEN THE WINDOWS AND DOORS, IT WILL JUST FLY OUTSIDE.
I COULD GET MY BUTTERFLY NET AND SCOOP IT UP!
IF IT LANDS, WE COULD THROW A PILLOWCASE OVER IT.
I WONDER IF THE BIRD KNOWS SANTA CLAUS...
?
HUH?
THE BIRD CAME DOWN THE CHIMNEY JUST LIKE SANTA, SO...
HEHEHEHE.
AUGHH!

OKAY, NO MORE WASTING TIME.
LET'S TRY OPENING THE WINDOWS AND DOORS!
DONE!
GO AHEAD, LITTLE BIRDIE.
...

GET OUT OF HERE, BIRD!!
IT WORKED!!
GOOD JOB! THANKS, MARGO.
Shut!
WHEW. ALL RIGHT, LET'S CLOSE EVERYTHING UP.
CLAUDIA!
OH MY GOSH!
VANESSA, WHAT HAPPENED?!

I DIDN'T KNOW YOU HAD A LOOSE TOOTH.
gross!
I DIDN'T KNOW, EITHER.
I WAS EATING A PIECE OF CANDY AND IT CAME OUT.

I'LL TAKE HER TO THE BATHROOM.
MALLORY, CAN YOU START MAKING DINNER WITH EVERYONE ELSE?
I WANT TUNA FISH SANDWICHES!!

gurgle gurgle

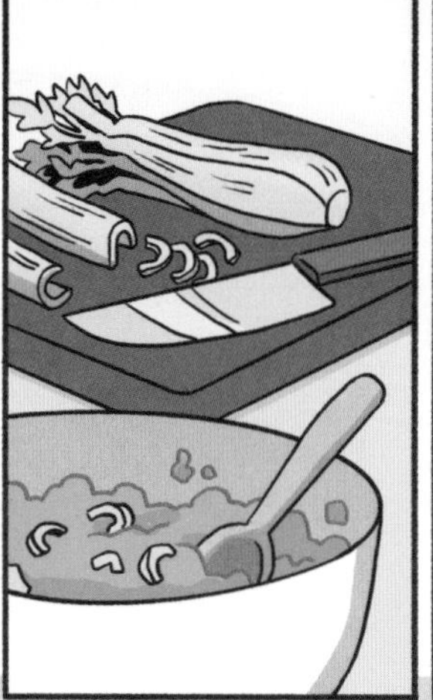

PHEW...

IF ANY OF US CLUB MEMBERS HAD DOUBTS ABOUT THE POWER OF THE CHAIN LETTER...

THEY WERE GONE AFTER CLAUDIA AND MAL'S SITTING EXPERIENCE.

WE WERE IN BIG TROUBLE. ALL OF US.

CHAPTER 9

THIS...IS AN EMERGENCY MEETING OF THE BABY-SITTERS CLUB.
YOU ALL KNOW WHY YOU'VE BEEN CALLED HERE.

BECAUSE OF ME.
BECAUSE I TEMPTED FATE AND THREW AWAY A CHAIN LETTER.

AND THEN HAD BEEN FORCED TO WEAR A BAD-LUCK CHARM... OR ELSE.

OR ELSE WHAT?
THE END OF CIVILIZATION AS WE KNOW IT?

SOMETHING MUST BE DONE ABOUT MARY ANNE'S, UM...

PROBLEM.

WELL, WE'VE GOT THE BOOKS. WE'D BETTER START GOING THROUGH THEM TO --
OH, WHAT'S THE WORD?

GET RID OF THE BAD STUFF?
COUNTERACT! A SPELL TO COUNTERACT THE BAD-LUCK CHARM IS OUR ONLY HOPE.

ALL RIGHT, LET'S START LOOKING.
TOOTSIE ROLL, ANYONE?
OMENS

MAGIC
& MORE
THERE'S A SPELL HERE FOR TURNING BAD LUCK TO GOOD LUCK. MAYBE THIS COULD WORK.
MAYBE!

WHAT DOES IT SAY?

LET'S SEE...TO REVERSE THE COURSE OF LUCK, PRESS A WHITE ROSE BETWEEN THE PAGES OF A BOOK OF SORCERY.
AFTER WAITING TWO MONTHS --
TWO MONTHS!
WHITE ROSE?
BOOK OF SORCERY??
WE DON'T HAVE A ROSE. WE DON'T HAVE A BOOK OF SORCERY.
AND WE CAN'T WAIT TWO MONTHS!
WELL, EXCUSE ME.
I CAN'T HELP WHAT THE BOOK SAYS.

HEY! HERE'S A LOVE SPELL!
A LOVE SPELL?
YEAH, YOU KNOW, TO GET THE PERSON YOU LIKE TO FALL FOR YOU.
ALL YOU NEED IS A LOCK OF THEIR HAIR, A FINGERNAIL CLIPPING...
CURSES
ONE OF THEIR EYELASHES --
MARY ANNE!
GIRLS?
EVERYTHING OKAY UP THERE?

YES, MOM!

KRISTY, I KNOW THIS IS SERIOUS, BUT PLEASE CALM DOWN, ALL RIGHT?
FINE.

CURSES

GOSH.
THERE'S A STORM COMING. LOOK AT THE SKY.

OOH, CREEPY.
CURSES
I THINK I FOUND SOMETHING --
BOOM
POTION

UM, ANYWAY...THIS SPELL DOESN'T EXACTLY COUNTERACT BAD LUCK, BUT IT'S SUPPOSED TO GET RID OF IT.
LET'S HEAR IT.
ON A PIECE OF PAPER, WRITE YOUR NAME, BIRTH DATE, ZODIAC SIGN, AND LUCKY NUMBER.
DAWN
Feb 5
11
OKAY...
PLACE THE PAPER IN AN AIRTIGHT GLASS CONTAINER BY AN ELM TREE ON THE NIGHT OF A FULL MOON.
WE COULD DO THAT!
THE NEXT MORNING, OPEN THE JAR, ADD TWO HAIRS FROM AN OX'S TAIL, SCRAPINGS FROM THE UNDERSIDE OF A SEA SNAKE --
ARE YOU MAKING THIS UP?

UNFORTUNATELY NOT.
CRACK!
!!
!!
!!
~DOOM
MAYBE WE'RE GOING ABOUT THIS ALL WRONG.
Y'KNOW, WE HAVEN'T EVEN FIGURED OUT WHO SENT THE BAD-LUCK CHARM.

IF WE KNEW, MAYBE WE COULD LOOK UP A SPELL TO PUT ON THEM.
LIKE A BAD-LUCK SPELL OR SOMETHING.
!

WHO SAYS SOMEONE SENT THE CHARM? IT JUST APPEARED.
THAT WAS PART OF YOUR BAD LUCK FROM THROWING OUT THE CHAIN LETTER.
BUT SOMEONE HAD TO SEND IT. IT CAME WITH A NOTE AND EVERYTHING.
THE QUESTION IS: WHO SENT IT AND WHY?
HMM, I SEE WHAT YOU MEAN.
LIKE, IS IT SOMEONE WE KNOW?
OR SOME EVIL AND UNKNOWN FORCE?
LIKE AN EVIL POWERMASTER?
AN EVIL POWERMASTER?!
YOU'RE SCARING ME, KRISTY.

IT COULD BE SOMETHING LIKE THAT, THOUGH.
RIGHT. I'VE WATCHED ENOUGH HORROR MOVIES TO KNOW.

CRCK!!
EEK!

MARY ANNE, DID YOU SAVE THE BOX THAT THE CHARM CAME IN? OR THE NOTE?
NO WAY.

DARN, THEY MIGHT HAVE CONTAINED CLUES TO WHO SENT IT...

SORRY...THEY'RE LONG GONE.
I THREW THEM OUT THE DAY I GOT THE CHARM.

SIIIGH.
WHY CAN'T THINGS BE SIMPLER?
LAST YEAR, MY BIGGEST CONCERN WAS WHO I WAS GOING WITH TO THE HALLOWEEN HOP.

HEY! DID I TELL YOU THAT I'M GOING WITH AUSTIN BENTLEY THIS YEAR?
YOU DIDN'T!
OOH!

WELL, I AM. BUT IT'S NO BIG DEAL. HE'S OKAY, I GUESS.

WHO ELSE IS GOING?
I'M GOING, BUT I DON'T HAVE A DATE. I DON'T NEED ONE TO HAVE FUN.
I'LL BE THERE WITH LOGAN.

MARY ANNE, IT'S SO NICE THAT YOU HAVE A STEADY BOYFRIEND. SOMEBODY YOU CAN COUNT ON.
EVEN BETTER THAT IT'S LOGAN!
HALF THE GIRLS IN OUR GRADE ARE HEAD OVER HEELS FOR HIM.
REALLY? LIKE WHO?
LIKE GRACE BLUME. TALK ABOUT A HUGE CRUSH.
SHE PROBABLY HATES HOW CLOSE WE ALL ARE TO HIM.
ORDINARILY, I MIGHT HAVE GLOATED ABOUT THAT, BUT WITH THE STORM AND ALL OUR OTHER PROBLEMS, I WASN'T IN THE MOOD.
THE NEWS ABOUT GRACE JUST FELT LIKE MORE BAD LUCK.

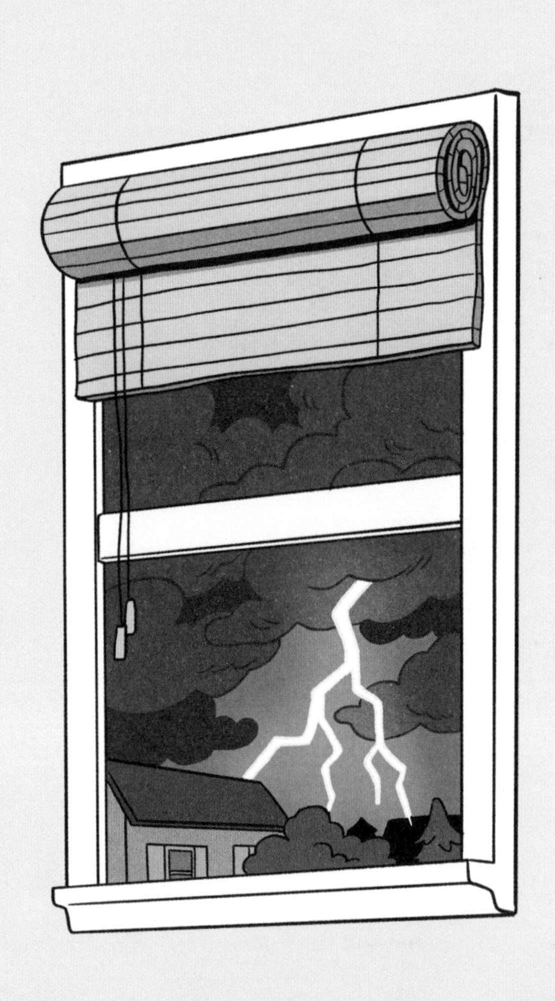

CHAPTER 10
OCTOBER 30, HALLOWEEN HOP NIGHT!
LOGAN AND I FINALLY DECIDED THAT WE WOULD DRESS UP.
WE'D BOTH WEAR COSTUMES INSPIRED BY *CATS*, A MUSICAL WE'D SEEN TOGETHER. ASIDE FROM RENTING THE HEADDRESSES, WE MADE EVERYTHING OURSELVES.

HOW DO I LOOK, TIGGER?
HISS
JUST LIKE YOU, HUH?
MROWR
AW, IT'S ONLY ME, YOU OLD FRAIDY-CAT!
ha
ha
ha

HEY, DAD.

!!

GRACIOUS, MARY ANNE. THAT IS SOME COSTUME. ESPECIALLY THAT FUR THING.
THANKS! I'LL TAKE THAT AS A COMPLIMENT.

WHY ARE YOU WEARING THAT NECKLACE?
THIS?

YES. IT TAKES AWAY FROM THE COSTUME A LITTLE.
OH, DOES IT? HA, I DON'T KNOW. I...I JUST LIKE IT.

WELL, ANYWAY.
YOU ARE ONE AMAZING CAT.

DING-DONG
THAT'S LOGAN!

HAVE FUN, MARY ANNE. BE HOME BY 10.
OKAY! SEE YOU LATER.

HEY!

YOUR COSTUME IS FANTASTIC!
THANKS!

ORDINARILY, DANCES MADE ME INCREDIBLY NERVOUS.
I COULD BE PRETTY SHY SOMETIMES...
SO I CLUNG TO LOGAN'S ARM AS WE WALKED UP TO THE DOOR.
HALLOWEEN HOP
IT HELPED HAVING LOGAN BY MY SIDE, BUT...

EEN HOP
I STILL FELT SO SELF-CONSCIOUS. WHAT IF EVERYONE STARED AT ME?
CHAMPS
HALLOWEEN HOP
BUT NOTHING HAPPENED. ONCE WE WERE INSIDE, I WAS ABLE TO RELAX A LITTLE.

HI, MARY ANNE!
HI, LOGAN!

HEY, GUYS!

GREAT COSTUMES. WHO MADE UP YOUR FACES?
WE DID THEM OURSELVES.
WOW!

LOOK WHO'S ALSO HERE.

COKIE AND GRACE?

THEY MAKE ME SO UNCOMFORTABLE.
OH, THEY JUST THINK THEY'RE BETTER THAN EVERYONE ELSE.

REALLY? THAT'S FUNNY. I ALWAYS THOUGHT **THEY** THOUGHT THAT **WE** THOUGHT WE WERE BETTER THAN EVERYONE ELSE.

WELL, WE ARE.

ha ha!

ALL RIGHT.
SHALL WE?

EXCUSE ME.
MIND IF WE SWITCH PARTNERS FOR A SONG?

OH.
HI, COKIE.
SURE.
CUTE COSTUME.
Y'KNOW, I DISAGREE WITH MY FRIENDS -- I DON'T THINK YOU LOOK RIDICULOUS AT ALL. AND NICE BAD-LUCK CHARM.
A YEAR AGO, A COMMENT LIKE THAT MIGHT HAVE MADE ME BURST INTO TEARS AND RUN HOME.
BUT THAT NIGHT, I SIMPLY WAITED UNTIL LOGAN WAS MY PARTNER AGAIN.

THEN LOGAN AND I DANCED THE NIGHT AWAY.
I DIDN'T EVEN TELL HIM ABOUT COKIE'S RUDE COMMENT.

GOOD NIGHT, LOGAN! GOOD NIGHT, MR. BRUNO!

Mary Anne Spier
MY HEART LEAPED INTO MY MOUTH.
BUT I SIMPLY WAVED TO LOGAN AND HIS DAD AGAIN.
I EVEN HAD A CHAT WITH DAD.
I DON'T KNOW HOW I MANAGED TO WAIT SO LONG BEFORE READING THE NOTE, BUT I DID.

To the girls in The Baby-sitters Club — Go to Old Man Hickory's headstone tomorrow at midnight to await your fate. Be there or beware.
OLD MAN HICKORY'S HEADSTONE WAS IN STONEYBROOK CEMETERY.
TOMORROW WAS HALLOWEEN.
AND TOMORROW NIGHT, THE MOON WOULD BE FULL.

CHAPTER 11
OCTOBER 31, HALLOWEEN.
2:09
I HARDLY SLEPT THAT NIGHT.
I'D JUST LAIN IN BED, JUMPING AT SOUNDS AND SHADOWS.
HOo
IT WAS A LONG, SPOOKY NIGHT.

I SPENT AN AWFUL LOT OF TIME ON THE PHONE THE NEXT MORNING.
WHICH WAS TRICKY, SINCE ONE OF THE HOUSE RULES IS THAT I CAN ONLY SPEND TEN MINUTES ON A PHONE CONVERSATION.

AND I HAD TO MAKE A LOT OF CALLS.
SO, AFTER I GOT BACK FROM THE HALLOWEEN HOP...
YEAH, THE NOTE LOOKS JUST LIKE THE ONE THAT CAME WITH THE CHARM.
EVERYONE HAD A LOT OF QUESTIONS.
OOPS, TEN MINUTES IS UP!

ring ring
HELLO?
IT'S KRISTY. I'M CALLING AN EMERGENCY CLUB MEETING.
ANOTHER ONE?

YES. THIS IS A CLUB MATTER, AND IT'S IMPORTANT.
WE'RE IN THIS TOGETHER, AND WE'LL DO SOMETHING ABOUT IT TOGETHER.
AYE, AYE, SIR!

THAT AFTERNOON, I ARRIVED AT CLAUDIA'S HOUSE WITH THE LETTER IN HAND.

KRISTY LOOKED DEAD SERIOUS.

SHE AND CLAUDIA READ THE NOTE.
AND AS THE OTHER MEMBERS ARRIVED...
THEY READ IT, TOO.
THEN KRISTY GOT RIGHT TO THE HEART OF THE MATTER.
WE'VE GOT TO DO THIS, YOU KNOW.

WE HAVE TO GATHER IN THE GRAVEYARD AT OLD HICKORY'S AT MIDNIGHT TONIGHT. JUST LIKE THE NOTE SAYS.
NO WAY!
UM, WHO'S OLD HICKORY?
HE WAS THIS MEAN OLD MAN WHO USED TO LIVE IN STONEYBROOK.
HIS NAME WAS JAMES HICKMAN. BUT EVERYONE CALLED HIM OLD HICKORY.
HE WAS THE RICHEST MAN IN TOWN. ALSO THE STINGIEST. AND A RECLUSE.
WHAT HAPPENED TO HIM?
THEY FOUND HIM IN HIS MANSION ONE DAY. HE WAS DEAD.

SOME PEOPLE SAY HE PASSED AWAY FROM OLD AGE.
OTHERS SAY IT WAS FROM MEANNESS.
HE NEVER WANTED HIS DEATH TO BE A BIG DEAL, NO FUNERAL OR ANYTHING.
BUT OLD HICKORY'S LONG-LOST NEPHEW, WHO RECEIVED HIS FORTUNE, FELT GUILTY AND HAD A GIANT HEADSTONE MADE.
MORE LIKE A STATUE.
YEAH, AND THE NEPHEW PUT IT UP IN THE GRAVEYARD.
SUPPOSEDLY, HIS SPIRIT WAS ANGRY BECAUSE HIS NEPHEW BURIED HIM IMPROPERLY.
AND NOW OLD HICKORY HAUNTS THE GRAVE AS A VENGEFUL SPIRIT.

AND WE'RE SUPPOSED TO GO TO A HAUNTED GRAVESTONE IN A CEMETERY?
AT MIDNIGHT ON HALLOWEEN? DURING A FULL MOON?!
WE ALL KNOW WHAT HAPPENS WHEN WE IGNORE WARNINGS.
I THINK WE BETTER.
BESIDES, I HAVE A FEELING SOMETHING IMPORTANT WILL HAPPEN IN THE GRAVEYARD.
LIKE EVERYTHING WILL GET CLEARED UP.
BUT WE HAVE TO BE TOGETHER ON THIS.
WE HAVE TO BE A TEAM.

SO, IF YOU'RE WILLING TO DO IT, RAISE YOUR HAND.
AND YOU'VE GOT TO MEAN IT.
raise
GREAT. WE'RE ALL IN, THEN.

NOW, HOW ARE WE ALL GOING TO SNEAK OUT OF OUR HOUSES TONIGHT?
WE SHOULD PROBABLY LEAVE AROUND 11:30.
SNEAK OUT?!
MY DAD'S THE LIGHTEST SLEEPER. I COULD NEVER GET AWAY WITH THAT!
OH, YOU'RE RIGHT. HMMM.
I GOT IT. WE'LL TELL OUR PARENTS THAT WE'RE HAVING A LATE-NIGHT HALLOWEEN SLUMBER PARTY!
AT MY HOUSE.
phew
DARN.
WHY DOES KRISTY ALWAYS HAVE SUCH GOOD IDEAS?

CHARLIE CAN PICK UP EACH OF YOU FROM YOUR HOUSES.
WE'LL TELL YOUR PARENTS THAT HE'S TAKING YOU TO MY HOUSE, BUT WE'LL GO TO THE GRAVEYARD INSTEAD.
AFTERWARD, WE REALLY WILL SPEND THE NIGHT AT MY HOUSE.
AND WE CAN CELEBRATE INTO THE NIGHT!
CELEBRATE WHAT?
MAKING IT OUT ALIVE.
CHARLIE CAN BE OUR GETAWAY DRIVER IN CASE ANYTHING GOES SOUTH. AND HE'LL BE ABLE TO KEEP THE SECRET.
DO YOU THINK YOU ALL CAN STICK TO THIS PLAN?

I DON'T KNOW WHY, BUT EVERY SINGLE ONE OF US NODDED.
ALL RIGHT.
IT'S SETTLED.
ASIDE FROM ASKING YOUR PARENTS ABOUT THE SLUMBER PARTY...
TELL NO ONE ABOUT TONIGHT.

BULLS
23

CHAPTER 12

TRICK OR TREAT!
IN THE HOURS THAT FOLLOWED, I HAD TO PRETEND EVERYTHING WAS FINE.
BOO
PRETEND THERE WASN'T A BAD-LUCK SPELL AND A BAD-LUCK CHARM.
AND THAT IN A FEW HOURS I WOULDN'T BE HANGING AROUND IN A GRAVEYARD LIKE A FOOL, WITH FIVE OTHER FOOLS...
WAITING FOR THE ANGRY GHOST OF OLD HICKORY TO APPEAR.
DING—DONG
IT WAS ALMOST IMPOSSIBLE.

AAAAAHHH!

-- AHHH HA HA HA, WHAT A GREAT COSTUME!
HAPPY HALLOWEEN!
??

I JUST WANT TO LOOK FORWARD TO MY NICE, COZY BED TONIGHT. NOT A COLD AND CREEPY GRAVEYARD.

I THOUGHT ABOUT CALLING LOGAN SIX DIFFERENT TIMES. BUT KRISTY'S WORDS ECHOED IN MY HEAD.
TELL NO ONE ABOUT TONIGHT.
eep!

IT DIDN'T HELP THAT DAWN AND I HAD RECENTLY WATCHED *NIGHT OF THE LIVING DEAD.*
I DIDN'T WANT TO MEET ANY OF THE LIVING DEAD IN STONEYBROOK CEMETERY.
I'D WATCHED A BUNCH OF HORROR MOVIES ON TV THIS WEEK, TOO.
I WOULDN'T BE SURPRISED IF, AT THE GRAVEYARD, A CLAMMY HAND REACHED OUT FROM THE BEYOND AND --

EEEEEEEK!!
MARY ANNE!
WHAT'S GOTTEN INTO YOU?
OH...
HI, DAD.
DINNERTIME.

UM...DAD?
YES?

KRISTY'S HAVING A SLUMBER PARTY TONIGHT FOR THE BABY-SITTERS CLUB.
IT'S A LATE ONE SO WE CAN, UM, ALL HELP WITH THE TRICK-OR-TREATERS FIRST. AND IT WAS A LAST-MINUTE IDEA, WHICH IS WHY I'M TELLING YOU NOW.
OH, AND YOU WON'T EVEN HAVE TO DRIVE ME! CHARLIE'S GOING TO! GREAT, RIGHT?

SO, UM... CAN I GO?

MAY I GO?

MAY I?
OF COURSE.
OH. THANK YOU!

THUD
!!
phew
MARY ANNE, PLEASE.
TELL ME WHAT'S WRONG. IS IT HALLOWEEN JITTERS?
UM...YEAH. YOU COULD SAY THAT.
AREN'T YOU A LITTLE OLD FOR THAT?
YOU KNOW THERE AREN'T ANY GHOULIES, GHOSTIES, OR THINGS THAT GO BUMP IN THE NIGHT, DON'T YOU?
WELL, I REALLY WASN'T TOO SURE.
DAD?
DO YOU BELIEVE IN BAD LUCK?

WELL, I --
BECAUSE A COUPLE WEEKS AGO I WAS, UM, DOWNTOWN AND SAW THIS NECKLACE AND THOUGHT IT WAS REALLY PRETTY. SO I BOUGHT IT.
BUT THEN THIS GIRL AT SCHOOL TOLD ME IT'S A BAD-LUCK CHARM.
SO I'M REALLY NERVOUS.
I'VE BEEN WEARING A BAD-LUCK CHARM FOR DAYS AND DAYS NOW.
WHY ARE YOU STILL WEARING IT?
GOOD QUESTION.
I DON'T KNOW.
I GUESS I'M AFRAID TO TAKE IT OFF.

MIND IF I TAKE A LOOK?
HMM.
WELL, I'LL BE.
MY GRANDMOTHER USED TO HAVE ONE OF THESE.
THIS ISN'T A BAD-LUCK CHARM, MARY ANNE.
DO YOU KNOW WHAT'S INSIDE THE GLASS?
WHAT?
IT'S A MUSTARD SEED.
A SYMBOL OF FAITH.

AFTER DINNER, I KEPT HANDING OUT CANDY AND DID SOME THINKING.
AT THE DANCE, COKIE THOUGHT THE MUSTARD SEED WAS A BAD-LUCK CHARM, TOO.
SHE'S JUST AS BIG AN IDIOT AS THE REST OF US!
BUT NONE OF US TOLD HER IT WAS A BAD-LUCK CHARM.
WHY WOULD SHE CALL IT THAT?
WE DIDN'T TELL ANYONE ABOUT IT. SO HOW WOULD SHE KNOW?
chew chew
UNLESS...
SHE HAD SOMETHING TO DO WITH IT?

DAD, I'M GOING TO MAKE A QUICK PHONE CALL!
SURE. I'LL ANSWER THE DOORBELL.

HELLO!

HI, KAREN. IT'S MARY ANNE. IS --
OH, MARY ANNE! WE JUST GOT BACK FROM TRICK-OR-TREATING. WE BROUGHT BACK A BUNCH OF CANDY.
MARY ANNE?
BUT WE ALSO GOT APPLES. GUESS WHO GAVE THEM TO US? MORBIDDA DESTINY! ISN'T THAT SPOOKY?!
OH, UM, YEAH.
CAN I SPEAK TO KRISTY? THIS IS REALLY IMPORTANT.
HERE, KAREN, GIVE ME THE PHONE.

DON'T TELL ME YOU CAN'T COME TONIGHT.
OH, I'LL BE THERE. NOW IT'S MORE IMPORTANT THAN EVER THAT WE GO.

I SHOWED THE CHARM TO MY FATHER, AND IT TURNS OUT THAT IT ISN'T A BAD-LUCK CHARM AT ALL.
YOU MEAN IT'S A **GOOD-LUCK** CHARM?!
NO, IT'S NOT EVEN A CHARM!

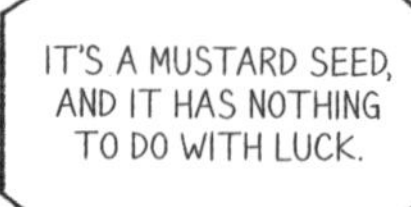

IT'S A MUSTARD SEED, AND IT HAS NOTHING TO DO WITH LUCK.
BUT YOU KNOW, LAST NIGHT AT THE DANCE, COKIE SAW IT AND CALLED IT A BAD-LUCK CHARM.
IF IT ISN'T A BAD-LUCK CHARM THAT EVERYONE KNOWS ABOUT, AND IF WE NEVER TOLD ANYONE, THEN WHY DID COKIE CALL IT ONE?

UNLESS...!
EXACTLY.

AHH, THAT DARN COKIE! SHE AND GRACE ARE SO...
THEY MAKE ME WANT TO **YELL**!!

OH!
OH!
I HAVE AN IDEA.
WE'VE GOT TO TELL THE OTHERS WHAT YOU FOUND OUT.
AND WE'LL NEED TO BRING SOME EXTRA THINGS TONIGHT.
BRING A MASK AND A FLASHLIGHT.
OH, AND...
KRISTY WAS OFF AND RUNNING WITH ANOTHER ONE OF HER FAMOUS IDEAS.

CHAPTER 13

JUST AS PLANNED, CHARLIE ARRIVED AT OUR HOUSE A LITTLE AFTER 10:30.

DO WE HAVE EVERYTHING?
I THINK SO.
I'VE GOT TWO FLASHLIGHTS, A MASK, A SHEET, AND THE STRING.

GREAT. I BROUGHT SOMETHING TO PLAY THE SOUND EFFECTS.
WE'RE GOING TO GET 'EM!
...ARE YOU SCARED?
TERRIFIED. YOU?
TERRIFIED, TOO.
BUT THERE'S NOTHING LIKE A LITTLE REVENGE.
HEHEHEEHE
HEY, YOU DIDN'T TELL LOGAN ABOUT THIS, DID YOU?
I DIDN'T, AND IT WASN'T EASY!

BUT IF I TOLD HIM, I KNEW HE'D WANT TO COME ALONG.
HE MIGHT HAVE EVEN TOLD OUR PARENTS AND WE WOULDN'T HAVE BEEN ABLE TO COME AT ALL.
THAT DOESN'T SOUND SO BAD...

OOPS, I MEAN...
GOOD JOB, MARY ANNE.

WE PICKED UP DAWN AND MALLORY.
AND THEN...
WE HEADED FOR THE GRAVEYARD.

PULL OVER HERE.
WAIT FOR US, ALL RIGHT?

REMEMBER EVERYTHING I TOLD YOU.
AND BE PREPARED TO GET HELP IF WE NEED IT.
YOU OWE ME FOR THIS.

OKAY.
LET'S GO TO OLD HICKORY'S.

HERE IT IS.
OLD HICKORY'S NEPHEW PLANTED THEM.
MORE STUFF HIS UNCLE DIDN'T WANT.
...MORE REASONS FOR HIM TO BE ANGRY.
OKAY. ENOUGH TALK. LET'S GET TO WORK.

HERE?
IT'S PITCH-BLACK! WHY ARE ALL THESE TREES HERE?
WE'LL RIG UP THE GHOSTS FIRST.

AOOOWO
clik
ALL RIGHT, IT'S 11:25.
LET'S GO OVER THE PLAN ONE MORE TIME.

I WAS SMOOSHED UP AGAINST OLD HICKORY'S GRAVE...
ON HALLOWEEN, NEAR MIDNIGHT...
UNDER A FULL MOON.
WHAT WERE WE DOING?

...CAN'T WAIT TO SEE THE LOOKS ON THEIR FACES.
PHWEEEEEE
KRISTY GAVE THE SIGNAL.

clik
OOOOOOHHHH
EEEEEEE
WH-WHAT WAS THAT?!

Cl
CK
AGH!!
AAAH!
HELP!!
AAAHHHHH
ooOOOOHOoVVUOH

I-IT'S THE GHOST OF OLD MAN HICKORY!
GAAAHAHAHAHAHAHAHA
1932-202
OH HELP.
OH HELP.
NOW!
AIIEEEEE
!!
AAAAAAHHHH

!!

BL
EH
YOU!

YOU LITTLE SNEAKS!
ARE YOU TALKING ABOUT US?
LOOK AT ALL THE THINGS YOU BROUGHT!
!
ARE YOU JUST UPSET WE BEAT YOU TO THE PUNCH?
WELL, THIS WASN'T WHAT I EXPECTED TO SEE TONIGHT.
CHARLIE!
I THOUGHT I TOLD YOU TO STAY IN THE CAR!

LOGAN?
MARY ANNE?
SOMEBODY BETTER EXPLAIN WHAT'S GOING ON HERE.
WELL, IT WON'T BE ME.
OR ME.
THEN I'LL TALK.
I WAS EATING A NICE, PLEASANT DINNER WHEN THE PHONE RANG.
THIS PERSON TOLD ME TO GO TO SOME OLD HICCUP'S GRAVE AT MIDNIGHT IF I WANTED TO SEE SOMETHING AMAZING.
I'M CURIOUS AND LIKE A LITTLE ADVENTURE, SO I AGREED.
WHEN I GOT TO THE CEMETERY, I RAN INTO CHARLIE THOMAS! HE DIRECTED ME TO THE GRAVE...

AND I FIND MY GOOD FRIENDS SCARING THE PANTS OFF YOU GUYS!
WHAT DID Y'ALL DO TO DESERVE THIS?
HA, TALK ABOUT SCARED.
YOUR GIRLFRIEND WAS THE ONE WHO WAS SCARED TO DEATH BY A LITTLE NECKLACE WE SENT HER.
SO YOU DID SEND IT!
THE CHAIN LETTER, TOO?
WHAT CHAIN LETTER?
BUT WHY?
WHY DID YOU SEND MARY ANNE THE CHARM AND ASK US TO COME HERE TONIGHT?

HMPH.
OH, WE MIGHT AS WELL JUST TELL THEM.
WE WANTED TO MAKE ALL OF YOU -- BUT ESPECIALLY MARY ANNE -- LOOK LIKE JERKS.
IT WASN'T COOL WHEN MARY ANNE EMBARRASSED US IN FRONT OF EVERYONE IN THE CAFETERIA.
IF WE SCARED YOU, WE COULD GET BACK AT YOU AND EMBARRASS MARY ANNE IN FRONT OF LOGAN.
I KNOW WHAT IT'S LIKE TO FEEL EMBARRASSED.
LIKE EVERYONE IS WATCHING AND JUDGING YOU.

I'M SORRY ABOUT WHAT HAPPENED IN THE CAFETERIA.
BUT EVEN SINCE BEFORE THEN, YOU'VE BEEN TALKING ABOUT US BEHIND OUR BACKS.
SAYING HURTFUL THINGS.
YEAH, JUDGING US WITHOUT KNOWING US.
BABY-SITTING ISN'T EASY, AND WE'RE GOOD AT OUR JOBS!
AND OUR KIDS AND THEIR PARENTS GENUINELY LIKE US.
WE'RE PROUD TO BE MEMBERS OF THE BABY-SITTERS CLUB.

AND COKIE, GRACE...
EVEN IF YOUR PRANK WORKED AND YOU SCARED MARY ANNE IN FRONT OF ME...
IT DOESN'T CHANGE THE FACT THAT SHE'S --
SHE'S MY G--
GIR--
ANYWAY, EVERYONE IN THE CLUB IS CARING AND KINDHEARTED.
I HOPE YOU CAN SEE THAT ONE DAY, TOO.
SO THERE.
C'MON, LET'S GO. CHARLIE'S WAITING.

AND WE HAVE SOME CELEBRATING TO DO.
WAIT.
YOU'RE NOT GOING TO...TELL ANYONE ABOUT THIS, ARE YOU?
WE WON'T.
BUT I HOPE THE NEXT TIME YOU HAVE A PROBLEM WITH SOMEONE, IT WON'T COME DOWN TO PRANKS AND TRICKS AND SCARING PEOPLE.

CHAPTER 14

GIRLS, COULD YOU KEEP IT DOWN?
THERE ARE SEVEN OTHER PEOPLE, PLUS A CAT AND A DOG, WHO ARE TRYING TO SLEEP.
SORRY, MOM!
ha ha!
YOU KNOW...
NOW THAT THE MYSTERY IS OVER, I THINK I'LL KEEP THE CHARM --
I MEAN, THE NECKLACE.

I LIKE KNOWING THAT IT'S A SYMBOL OF FAITH.
IT REMINDS ME OF LOGAN AND ME. WE'RE FAITHFUL TO EACH OTHER.

CUTE

WHAT IS IT, JESSI?
SOMETHING'S BEEN BOTHERING ME.

COKIE AND GRACE WERE BEHIND THE NECKLACE AND CUTOUT NOTES.

BUT COKIE SAID THEY DIDN'T SEND THE CHAIN LETTER.

YOU'RE RIGHT...
MAYBE THERE IS GOOD AND BAD LUCK AFTER ALL...
MAYBE COKIE AND GRACE WERE MY BAD LUCK.
IF I HADN'T BROKEN THE CHAIN, MAYBE THEY NEVER WOULD HAVE TRIED TO TRICK US.
WHOA.
I WONDER HOW LONG BAD LUCK LASTS...
MAYBE WE NEED A SPELL AFTER ALL. SHOULD WE CHECK THE LIBRARY BOOKS?
I HAD TO RETURN THEM. THEY WERE OVERDUE.

WELL, WE COULD MAKE UP OUR OWN SPELL.
HERE, MARY ANNE, LET ME PULL OUT ONE OF YOUR EYELASHES --
NO WAY!!
HA HA HA!
YOU KNOW, EVEN IF BAD LUCK DID VISIT US AFTER THE LETTER, I THINK IT'S OVER NOW.
THOSE OF US WHO WENT TO THE DANCE HAD FUN.
AND WE PULLED A GOOD TRICK ON GRACE AND COKIE. OUR LUCK IS CHANGING.
I GOT AN EIGHTY-FIVE ON MY MATH TEST.

I FOUND MY LOST WATCH!
ONE OF MY FAVORITE AUTHORS IS DOING AN EVENT IN STAMFORD SOON.
MY BROTHER'S GETTING A'S AT HIS NEW SCHOOL IN CALIFORNIA.

MY BALLET TEACHER TOLD ME I'M ONE OF HER BEST STUDENTS EVER.
THEN IT'S OVER.

NO MATTER WHERE THE CHAIN LETTER CAME FROM...THE BAD-LUCK MYSTERY IS OVER.

WE CAN STOP BEING WITCHES AND GO BACK TO BEING BABY-SITTERS!

KR
AK!
UH-OH.

OH NO, MARY ANNE!
YOU KNOW WHAT THAT MEANS, RIGHT? SEVEN YEARS OF BAD LUCK!

HA HA!
WELL, I CAN TAKE IT.
I'VE DECIDED THAT SINCE MY MUSTARD SEED IS A SYMBOL OF FAITH, WE'RE PROTECTED.

SO GO AHEAD. BREAK ALL THE MIRRORS YOU WANT!
ha ha ha!

ANN M. MARTIN'S The Baby-sitters Club is one of the most popular series in the history of publishing — with more than 190 million books in print worldwide — and inspired a generation of young readers. Her novels include *Belle Teal, A Corner of the Universe* (a Newbery Honor book), *Here Today, A Dog's Life,* and *On Christmas Eve,* as well as the much-loved collaborations, *P.S. Longer Letter Later* and *Snail Mail No More,* with Paula Danziger, and *The Doll People* and *The Meanest Doll in the World,* written with Laura Godwin and illustrated by Brian Selznick. Ann lives in upstate New York.